Cold

Written by Brylee Gibson

Rigby

Cold Places

At the ends of the earth are two very cold
and windy places. One is a big frozen
land, and one is a big frozen land and ocean.
These two places have long winters
and short summers.

The Arctic

The Arctic is at the north end
of the earth. Much of it is covered
in ice and snow that never melts.
Trees cannot grow in the Arctic
because it is too cold and windy,
but some small plants do grow there.
They have long roots that go deep down
and help them hold on when it is windy.

moss pinks

Arctic

Some animals like the snowy owl and the arctic fox live in the Arctic. The arctic fox has brown fur in the summer, but in the winter the fur grows thick and white. Some birds like the arctic tern fly away in the winter and come back in the summer.

snowy owl

arctic tern

arctic fox

7

Some people live in the Arctic.
These people live in houses, but when they go
hunting, they stay in houses made of ice.
This kind of house is called an igloo.
An igloo is made from big blocks of ice.

Antarctica

Antarctica is at the south end of the earth. Not many plants grow in Antarctica, and it is so cold that if a cup of boiling water were thrown in the air, it would freeze before it hit the ground. Antarctica is called a frozen desert because it never rains.

Antarctica

Antarctica is so cold and so far away from other lands that not many animals live there. But in the summer, penguins, whales, and walruses go to Antarctica for food, and to have their babies.

whale

walrus

The only people who live in Antarctica are the people who go there to work. They want to find out more about it and the animals that live there. The weather is so cold that they have to wear very warm clothes and special boots. Some of the boots have air inside them. When the people go on a plane, they let the air out so the boots don't explode!

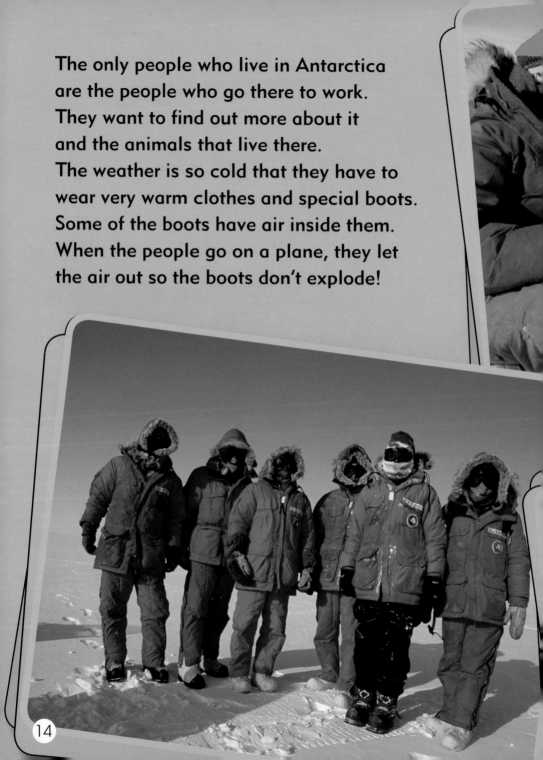

Average temperature
in Antarctica

140°F
104°F
68°F
Water
freezes
32°F
4°F
-40°F
-76°F

People who work in Antarctica live in buildings. Some are built on top of the ice, but some are built under it. Sometimes the ice moves and the buildings under the ground break up. New ones have to be built so the people can keep working there.

inside the dome at Amundsen-Scott South Pole Station

the dome entrance at Amundsen-Scott South Pole Station

the British Antarctic Survey research station at Halley, in Antarctica

The Arctic is at the north end of the earth.

The Arctic

Some small plants grow in the Arctic.

Antarctica is at the south end of the earth.

Antarctica

Not many plants grow in Antarctica.

Some animals
live in
the Arctic.

Some people
live in
the Arctic.

Not many
animals live in
Antarctica.

People do not live
in Antarctica,
but some go there
to work.

Index

Guide Notes

Title: Cold Places
Stage: Launching Fluency – Orange

Genre: Nonfiction
Approach: Guided Reading
Processes: Thinking Critically, Exploring Language, Processing Information
Written and Visual Focus: Maps, Photographic Sequence, Graph, Labels, Index
Word Count: 388

THINKING CRITICALLY
(sample questions)
- What do you know about places that are cold?
- What might you expect to see in this book?
- Look at the index. Encourage the students to think about the information and make predictions about the text content.
- Look at pages 4 and 5. Why do you think the ice and snow never melts in the Arctic?
- Look at pages 6 and 7. How do you think having white fur would help the arctic fox in the winter?
- Look at pages 8 and 9. Why do you think an igloo is made in a circular shape?
- Look at pages 10 and 11. Why do you think it never rains in Antarctica?
- Look at pages 12 and 13. These animals visit Antarctica in the summer for food. Where do you think they go in the winter for their food?
- What things in the book have helped you understand the information?
- What questions do you have after reading the text?

EXPLORING LANGUAGE

Terminology
Photograph credits, index

Vocabulary
Clarify: Arctic, Antarctica, ocean, melts, igloo, walruses, buildings
Singular/Plural: place/places, winter/winters, root/roots
Homonyms: two/too/to, there/their, break/brake

Print Conventions
Apostrophes – contraction (don't)